~ For David . . . a promise fulfilled ~

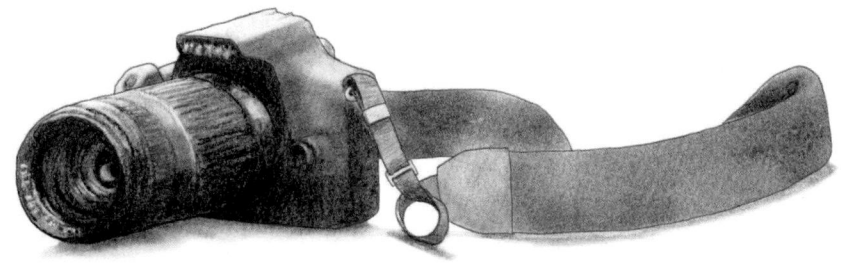

© 2021 Vicki S. Risbeck and Sonburst Books, LLC

All rights reserved. No part of this publication may be reproduced, distributed, or transmitted in any form or by any means, including photocopying, recording, or other electronic or mechanical methods, without the prior written permission of the publisher, except in the case of brief quotations embodied in critical reviews and certain other noncommercial uses permitted by copyright law. For permission requests, contact: **vsrisbeck@sonburstbooks.com**

ISBN 978-1-09838-031-1

This is a work of fiction. Any resemblance to actual events or persons, living or dead, is entirely coincidental.

Printed in the United States of America by Sonburst Books, LLC.

First Edition

A Lens View 📷 Family

By

Vicki Burris Risbeck

Photographs By

Robert Charles McAdams

Illustrations By

Dixie Whitlatch Carrier

Well, it's officially Daxter E. Roland Jr., named after my father. He's the only other Daxter I know. But everyone calls me Dax, and I really like my name. It's who I am. I like soccer (I play right guard), reading fantasy books, using my tablet for everything, and eating. I really love eating! Pizza is my favorite, and of course I love ice cream. But I have a new favorite. At Easter we had pickled beets and hard-boiled eggs. I loved them! Food and I are buddies for sure.

I live with my mom, my little sister Isabella, my dog Murphy, and my Papaw Dean. He is my Mom's father and has lived with us since Mamaw Dean died a few years ago. That was a very sad time. Papaw is a real buddy of mine, and I think he is very wise, too.

Mom is a social worker and works with kids who don't live with their parents because they can't take care of them properly. She loves her job, but it makes her sad sometimes. On the days she works late, we stay with Papaw. It's always an adventure! We play games, and I love having him around to listen to his stories about growing up and when Mom was young.

This is Isabella. We call her Bella most of the time except when she gets in trouble with Mom or Dad. Then it is "ISABELLA MAE!" I sometimes call her Whiz because she is always on the move. She's in kindergarten and has a lot of friends there. She also takes ballet, but sometimes struggles with directions. She is one funny girl!

She loves to play with bugs and worms and has a pet Bearded Dragon named Stretch. But she doesn't like to eat everything like I do. If it's milk and cookies, great. But do NOT try giving her pickled beets and eggs ~ she will spit them right back at you.

The best thing about Bella is she wants to be a pilot when she grows up and says she will take me all over the world to explore. That will be fun, but I hope she learns to eat something other than milk and cookies before then! She is pretty cool for a little sister.

I live with my dad some of the time, too. Mom and Dad got divorced a few years ago and share custody of Bella and me. At first it was really sad and hard not seeing both of them all of the time. Now I think we are lucky because we have two homes ~ and two families. Our houses and neighborhoods are different, but both are great. At Dad's we have a cat named Jewel and a hamster named Nicholas. Nicholas keeps us on our toes because he always finds a way to escape his cage. Jewel just watches him. Dad got married to Miss Julie last summer. We have known her for a long time because she was our preschool teacher.

They were married in a park with beautiful roses, and I was his best man. Bella was the flower girl, and she did well until she saw a huge bug on one bush and forgot to throw the petals. It was a nice wedding though, and we love having Miss Julie as our stepmother. Although now, we call her JJ. We just found out we are going to have a baby brother or sister in a few months. We are so excited! Dad and JJ say they don't care if it's a boy or girl as long as it's healthy. Mom is happy for them. She says, "Family is family."

I turned ten on my last birthday. We had a party at Mom's house. Most of my friends came, including my best friend Silas. Silas is my next-door neighbor, and we have been best buddies since preschool. He is the goalie on our soccer team, and we take turns spending the night at each other's house. We play a lot of Zombie Warriers from Space on our tablets and eat lots of pizza. Mom says we are like twins!

I got a lot of presents that day, but my favorite one was from Papaw. He gave me my own camera! It wasn't a big one like his, but he said I need to grow into a bigger one, whatever that means. You see, Papaw was a photographer when he worked, and he had his own shop. He retired right after Mamaw died and moved in with us. He still takes pictures all the time, though. I love to go with him when he goes to take them so I can see what he sees. He always says, "A picture is worth a thousand words."

Last week in the car on the way back to Mom's, I heard Dad and JJ talking about how when the baby comes, their family tree will be a little more complicated. I try and understand what grown-ups mean, but sometimes it is hard. I didn't get a chance to ask him then, so when I went to Mom's, I asked Papaw what that meant. Papaw and I talk about everything. Were they buying a tree for the baby? And how could a tree be complicated? Papaw smiled and pulled out a pad of paper and drew two sketches, while I imagined how my family with Dad and JJ would look.

He explained that the first one was what a family tree would look like if my parents had stayed married. Then he said the second one was what it will look like with the new baby. I looked closely. It didn't matter much to me that Bella and I were on different branches from the baby, because we were on the same tree. Papaw said, "Blended together, you make one beautiful family."

I asked him why they call it a family tree though. How did they come up with that idea? Papaw smiled and said the words he always says to me before we look at his pictures.

"Well . . . let me show you!"

All trees have roots that secure them, even when their branches grow in many different directions. The roots keep them strong and help them grow.

"Just like families," Papaw said. "Your mom and dad may have grown in different directions, but they created roots in you and Bella that will always remain the same."

Some trees either start out small, or stay small, but they still remain trees. That doesn't change. Some grow very large and extend their branches out a long way.

"Just like some families. Whether small or large, they are still family. And the closer the family, the more strength it has. This happens through blood - like your mom and dad and you and Bella - or through love, like you three and JJ."

He looked at me to see if I was understanding.

"So, when your baby brother or sister arrives, you will be an even stronger family because of all the love you share."

Some trees are very colorful, looking bright and happy, while others may appear dark and worn ~ and even scarred.

"Just like some families have great joy, while others may have hard times come upon them."

It was starting to make sense to me.

"Like the families Mom works with," I responded, thinking about how those families were torn apart.

Papaw smiled and nodded.

Trees can become burdened down with heavy loads that make them bend and break at times.

Papaw was quiet as he showed me the next photos.

"Just like families who, at times, deal with pain and sorrow."

Papaw was again quiet, and his eyes looked sad.

"Like when Mamaw was sick and died?" I whispered.

He nodded and said in a solemn voice, "Yes. Just like that."

The good news is that trees also have the ability to bring forth new life, bear fruit, and attract life to them.

He showed me several more photos.

But when Papaw started to talk this time, I jumped in before he had a chance to continue.

"I get it!" I burst out. "Like Dad and JJ with the new baby coming, right? How we are all so happy and excited for him or her to be part of us? Part of our new family tree?"

I looked at Papaw, who was smiling broadly.

Trees, like families, provide shade and shelter for the storms of life as we make our way through this world.

"No matter what Dax, trees have been around since the beginning of time and so have families. They are everlasting."

"So, Dax, do you understand more about family trees now," Papaw asked, putting his arm around me. He paused. It was my turn to nod.

"Sure do, thanks. You are one great photographer ~ and one wise man!" And I was off to think about what I had learned from him that day. I can't wait for another lens view with Papaw!

The Team

Vicki Burris Risbeck is a life-long educator, serving in many capacities for the last forty-five years. She holds a Bachelor of Arts degree from Capital University, a Master's degree in Guidance and Counseling from The Ohio State University, and a Doctorate degree in Educational Theory and Practice ~ with a cognate in Reading ~ also from The Ohio State University. This is her first published children's book, where her goal is for parents and teachers to share the joy, pain, and wonderment of life together through reading. *A Lens View ~ Family* is the first in a series of discovery books using authentic photography and beautiful illustrations. Visit her at www.sonburstbooks.com for more information, updates, ordering, and a special corner for parents and teachers with tips on how to enrich the reading experience for children.

Dixie Whitlatch Carrier is an award-winning artist with many years of creating images to tell a story. She credits the Columbus College of Art & Design (CCAD) for nourishing her passion for illustration, portrait work, painting, and landscape design. Dixie looks forward to each new project with eagerness and joy.

Robert Charles McAdams is a husband, father of five, and grandfather of nine. He has been taking photos since 3rd grade, and each day brings him the excitement of taking more. He is a 1980 graduate of The Ohio State University and a Viet Nam Veteran. "I am very proud to have been invited to be a part of this project," says Bob.